Published exclusively for
J Sainsbury plc
Stamford Street, London SE1 9LL
by William Heinemann Ltd
an imprint of Reed Children's Books
Michelin House, 81 Fulham Road, London SW3 6RB
and Auckland, Melbourne, Singapore and Toronto

Illustrations by Arkadia

Printed in Italy

ISBN 0 434 96493 X

THOMAS *and the Race*

Based on The Railway Series by the Rev. W. Awdry

SAINSBURY · HEINEMANN

Here comes Thomas the Tank Engine.
He pulls his coaches up and down the line.

One day Bertie the Bus said to Thomas, “I can go faster than you. Let’s have a race to the top station.”

The Stationmaster said, “Are you ready? Go!”
“Faster, faster,” called Annie and Clarabel.
“Bertie is in front.”

ELSBRIDGE
1

But Thomas did not hurry.
He knew what was ahead.

It was the level crossing.
The gates were closed.

Bertie had to wait while Thomas raced past.
But then Thomas had to stop at a station.

“Quickly, please!” he called to the passengers.

Thomas saw Bertie racing over the bridge.

Thomas hurried along to catch up.
He puffed and puffed.
Bertie was held up at the traffic lights.

Thomas whooshed into the top station just ahead of Bertie. "Well done," said the passengers and the Fat Controller. And everyone cheered.

1